Disney's

Storybook

COLLECTION

Ladybird

TABLE OF CONTENTS

TABLE OF CONTENTS

Edited by Nancy Parent
Designed by Todd Taliaferro

10 9 8 7 6 5 4 3 2 1

A catalogue record for this book is available from the British Library.

Published by Ladybird Books, Ltd.
80 Strand, London WC2R 0RL

A Penguin Company

LADYBIRD and the device of a ladybird are trademarks of Ladybird Books, Ltd.

Printed in Spain by Gráficas Estella, S. A.

www.ladybird.co.uk

Walt Disney's

Snow White
and the Seven Dwarfs

Long ago, in a faraway place, there lived a lovely princess named Snow White. Her hair was black as coal, her lips red as rose, and her skin as white as snow.

Snow White's stepmother, the Queen, was very cruel.

She hated anyone who was more beautiful than she. The Queen treated Snow White like a servant.

Snow White never complained. She was obedient and hard-working, but she dreamed of a handsome prince who would take her away to his castle. One day, while drawing water from the well, a handsome stranger did appear, charmed by Snow White's singing. But Snow

White was too shy to speak to him.

Inside the castle, the Queen asked her magic mirror, "Mirror, mirror, on the wall, who is the fairest of them all?"

Every day the mirror had the same reply. "You are the fairest," it told her. And the Queen was content for another day.

But as Snow White grew older, she also grew more

beautiful. The Queen became very jealous.

One day the magic mirror told the Queen that someone else was the fairest in the land. It was the princess, Snow White!

In a jealous rage, the Queen called her royal huntsman into the throne room.

"Take Snow White far into the forest and kill her," she commanded. "And as proof of your deed, bring

me back her heart in this." She handed the stunned

huntsman a beautiful carved box.

The hunter looked at the innocent Princess. "I cannot

kill you," he said. "You

must hide!" He put an

animal's heart in the box to

give to the Queen instead.

Snow White ran off

through the dark woods.

At last she came to a

cottage. "Who lives here?"

Snow White wondered.

Then she heard voices singing in the distance.

The seven dwarfs who lived in the cottage were coming

home from a hard day at work in the diamond mine.

The dwarfs introduced themselves. Their names were Sleepy, Grumpy, Happy, Doc, Dopey, Sneezy, and Bashful.

They invited Snow White to share their supper.

Snow White felt so safe with the dwarfs that she decided to stay with them.

But the evil Queen soon found out that Snow White was still alive. She would have to take matters into her own wicked hands.

She fled to a dungeon beneath the castle. There the Queen mixed a potion to change her into an old hag. Then she took an apple and dipped it into some poison. "One bite of this apple and Snow White will close her eyes forever!" she cackled.

The old woman appeared at Snow White's window. "Hello, dear," she smiled. "Taste one of my delicious apples." She held the poisoned apple out to Snow White.

The birds tried to warn Snow White away from the poisoned fruit. "Stop it! Stop it!" cried Snow White.

But it was too late. Snow White took a big bite from the apple, and straight away fell to the ground. The animals  of the forest ran to the dwarfs to warn them that something was very wrong and they needed to come home straightaway!

The seven dwarfs raced to the cottage and found the old woman trying to creep away and Snow White lying lifeless on the floor. The dwarfs chased the hag into the forest.

A storm began to blow as the evil woman ran away.

She came to the edge of a steep and rocky cliff and tried

to move a huge rock so it would roll down on top of the

poor dwarfs and crush them.

"Look out!" cried Grumpy to the others.

At that moment, lightning struck. The Queen lost her balance and fell to her doom!

The sad little dwarfs built a bed of gold and glass for their beloved Snow White. They kept watch over her, day and night.

One day a handsome prince rode into the forest and saw Snow White lying on her bed of glass and gold. How beautiful she was! The Prince knelt down and kissed Snow White tenderly.

His kiss awakened her. Snow White opened her eyes and immediately fell in love with the Prince. He took her in his arms and together they rode off to his kingdom, where they lived happily ever after.

WALT DISNEY'S

Pinocchio

Once upon a time, Geppetto the woodcarver made a special puppet that he named Pinocchio. "I wish you were a real boy," said Geppetto, sadly.

That night the Blue Fairy came to Geppetto's

workshop. "Good Geppetto," she said, "you have made others so happy, you deserve to have your wish come true."

Smiling, the Blue Fairy touched the puppet gently with her wand. "Little puppet made of pine, wake! The gift of life be thine!" In the blink of an eye, she had brought Pinocchio to life.

"Pinocchio, if you are brave, honest and unselfish, you will be a real boy one day," said the Blue Fairy.

Then she turned to Jiminy Cricket. "Jiminy," she said, "you must help Pinocchio." She told Jiminy that she was giving him a very important job. He must be Pinocchio's conscience – keeper of the knowledge of right and wrong.

The next day Geppetto proudly sent his little wooden boy off to school. "Jiminy Cricket will show you the way," said Geppetto. "Make sure you go straight there!"

Pinocchio headed off, but never found his way to

school. He met Stromboli, an evil puppeteer, who promised to make him famous. Pinocchio happily agreed to perform for him. That night he had great fun as he danced on the stage for his new friend. But afterwards Stromboli locked him in a cage.

The Blue Fairy appeared and asked Pinocchio why he hadn't gone to school. Pinocchio lied and told her he had been kidnapped. Suddenly his nose began to grow.

When Pinocchio finally told the truth, the fairy set him free. "I'll forgive you this once, Pinocchio. But this is the last time I can help you. Remember, a boy who won't be good might just as well be made of wood!"

The next day Pinocchio met a man who drove a stagecoach pulled by a team of donkeys. "Come to Pleasure Island!" said the coachman. The stagecoach was full of noisy boys. Pinocchio thought it looked like fun.

"Don't go, Pinoke!" cried Jiminy Cricket, but still Pinocchio climbed aboard, ready for adventure.

On Pleasure Island, Pinocchio and the other boys ran wild and stuffed themselves with sweets. But Pinocchio's fun did not last long. All of a sudden, he began to grow donkey ears and a tail!

Pinocchio was frightened. He and Jiminy Cricket ran for their lives, away from Pleasure Island.

But when the two returned home, Geppetto was gone. Pinocchio was very upset. Where could Geppetto be? A dove suddenly appeared with a note.

The note said Gepetto had gone to sea to look for Pinocchio and been swallowed by Monstro, the whale.

Pinocchio set off at once to find Monstro and save his father. And indeed, Pinocchio found Geppetto in the belly of the great whale. Geppetto was thrilled to see his little puppet. But how were they ever going to get home?

Pinocchio had an idea. Together, they built a fire and used

the smoke to make Monstro sneeze.

Geppetto and Pinocchio were thrown out of the whale

and into the sea. Fighting the waves, Pinocchio helped his

father to shore safe and sound. But then he just crumpled

and lay face-down in the water! Geppetto scooped

Pinocchio up in his arms and carried him home.

Geppetto laid Pinocchio on his bed and knelt by his side.

"Little Pinocchio, you risked your life to save me," he sobbed.

Suddenly the Blue Fairy appeared once more.

Waving her magic wand over Pinocchio, she said, "Now
you have proved to be brave, truthful, and unselfish.
Today you will become a real boy. Awake, Pinocchio!"

Jiminy Cricket watched as his friend came to life.
Their troubles were over and Jiminy's job was done.
At last, Geppetto's wish for a real son had come true.

Walt Disney's
Bambi

One beautiful spring morning a little rabbit named Thumper woke Friend Owl with some wonderful news. A baby deer had been born deep in the woods.

"A new prince is born!" cried the little rabbit.

All the other animals rushed to see for themselves.

"What's his name?" they asked his mother.

"Why, his name is Bambi," she replied.

Soon Bambi met all the creatures in the forest. First Mrs Quail and her

babies stopped to say hello. Then Mrs Opossum and her family, who liked to hang upside down, smiled at Bambi. Next, a mole poked his head out from the ground to wish

Bambi a good morning. Even a flock of little bluebirds flew down to greet the young prince.

Bambi made friends with Thumper and a shy little

skunk called Flower. They laughed and played together every day. Soon, at the pond in the meadow, Bambi made another friend – a playful girl fawn named Faline.

Summer and autumn passed happily for Bambi, and when the winter came, Thumper taught Bambi how to spin and slide on the frozen pond. Bambi had never done anything like this before. They had so much fun playing together. Bambi didn't want it ever to end.

Finally winter was over and the spring brought many changes. Bambi had grown into a handsome young buck.

His friends Thumper and Flower had grown up, too. Friend Owl was sure that any moment now they would all meet somebody and fall in love.

The three friends laughed at the wise old owl and

agreed to spend all their time together – until Flower met a lovely girl skunk and spent all his time with her. Bambi knew he would miss Flower. But at least he still had Thumper. Then Thumper fell in love, too!

Next it was Bambi's turn. Soon he met a beautiful doe in the meadow. It was his old friend Faline! Bambi suddenly felt dizzy and light as a feather! Bambi and Faline frolicked together just as they had done in the meadow when they were young.

But Bambi wasn't the only buck who liked Faline. A stag named Ronno soon pushed his way between them challenging Bambi to a fierce fight. Bambi charged Ronno with all his might and the two bucks butted heads again and again. Finally, Bambi won the fight. And from that day on, he and Faline were always together.

One autumn morning
Bambi smelled something
strange – smoke. Just
then a majestic stag
appeared. It was Bambi's
father, the Great Prince.
"The forest is on fire!"
he cried. "Hurry! We
must warn the other

animals to run to the river island."

Bambi and the Prince warned all the forest animals.

Then they crossed the river, where they found Faline

waiting for them. Bambi and his friends watched as fire

destroyed their forest homes.

After the fire was out, the old stag turned to Bambi.

"I must leave you now," he said. "You will take my place

as Prince of the Forest." Bambi knew this was a great

responsibility, but he was ready to accept it.

Gradually, the smoke disappeared and the animals began to rebuild their homes.

Autumn once again turned into winter and winter into

spring. The forest was lush and green and smelled of blooming flowers.

Soon Thumper and his little bunnies were waking Friend Owl once again. Faline had given birth to twin fawns. All the animals proudly came to celebrate.

But no one was prouder than Bambi, the new Prince of the Forest.

He stood overlooking the thicket, smiling down on his family, his heart filled with love. Soon, Bambi would teach them the lessons of the forest that he himself had learned so long ago.

WALT DISNEY'S

Cinderella

Once upon a time, there was a pretty young girl named Cinderella. Everyone loved Cinderella because she was good and sweet and kind.

But Cinderella's widowed father believed she needed a mother. So he married again to a woman with two

daughters of her own. Soon Cinderella's father died and she was left to live with her mean stepmother and two jealous stepsisters in the attic of their house.

Poor Cinderella had to do all the cooking and cleaning. She no longer had nice things and wore only tattered old clothes, while her stepmother and step-sisters had beautiful clothes and lived very comfortably.

But no matter how cruel her stepmother

and stepsisters were, Cinderella was always cheerful. Even the little animals loved to be near her. She made friends with the mice and birds, making them little clothes to wear and caring for them. Two of Cinderella's best friends were Jaq and Gus. Cinderella and Jaq were always saving Gus from old Lucifer the cat, who had his eye on the plump little mouse.

One day a

letter came inviting everyone to the palace for a ball.

Cinderella was so excited but her stepmother said,

"Cinderella may only go to the ball if she finishes her

work." Cinderella happily scrubbed the floors, washed

and ironed, working as quickly as she could.

Meanwhile, Cinderella's little friends went to work making her a lovely gown. The birds and mice who loved Cinderella so much wanted to surprise her. When she saw what they had done, she gasped with joy. Cinderella put on the beautiful dress, kissed her friends and ran downstairs to join her stepsisters.

The birds and mice had used sashes, ribbons and

beads that belonged to Cinderella's stepsisters and when they saw the gown, and how beautiful Cinderella looked, they tore it to shreds.

"That's my ribbon!" cried one.

"And those are my beads!" yelled the other.

Cinderella ran to the garden in tears.

"Don't cry, child," said a gentle voice. "I am your Fairy

Godmother, and I have come to help you."

The Fairy Godmother waved her wand. Four mice

became four white horses, and a big, round pumpkin

became a glittering coach.

Again the Fairy Godmother waved her wand and turned Cinderella's torn dress into a beautiful gown.

"Now you shall go to the ball Cinderella," she smiled. "But you must leave by midnight. After that, the magic spell will be broken."

At the ball, the Prince danced with Cinderella all evening.

She felt as if she were dreaming! The King was delighted

to see the Prince looking so happy.

Suddenly, the clock was striking midnight and

Cinderella ran from the palace. She was in such a hurry

that she left one glass slipper behind. The Prince ran after her, but it was too late.

Next day, the Prince sent the Grand Duke to find the young woman who had lost her slipper. When he got to Cinderella's house, both stepsisters tried on the glass slipper,

but their feet were much too big.

Cinderella's stepmother told the Grand Duke that there were no other ladies in the house. She had locked Cinderella in her room. But Cinderella's little friends, Gus and Jaq, stole the key, opened her door and freed

Cinderella just in time.

When Cinderella rushed downstairs and asked if she could try on the slipper, her stepmother was furious, and tripped the footman so that the

glass slipper fell to the floor and shattered.

But all was not lost. Cinderella reached into her pocket and pulled out the matching shoe. It was a perfect fit!

The Grand Duke was happy and relieved that he had found the slipper's owner. The Prince would be married at last. And Cinderella's dreams would all come true.

WALT DISNEY'S

ALICE
in
WONDERLAND

One beautiful spring day a young girl named Alice
sat by the river listening to her sister read aloud
from a book. But Alice wasn't really listening.

She was playing with her cat, Dinah, and daydreaming.

The sun was bright and the air was warm. Soon Alice
began to close her eyes. She no longer heard her sister's voice.

Suddenly a large
white rabbit dashed by.
Alice jumped up. The
rabbit was wearing a
waistcoat and bow tie
and was carrying a huge

pocket watch. "I'm late! I'm late for a very important date," the White Rabbit muttered as he went along.

Alice went chasing after him, but stopped short at a rabbit hole.

The rabbit scuttled down the hole. Thinking he might

be late for something fun, like a party, Alice followed him and suddenly realised she was falling head over heels, down and down. But as she fell, instead of going faster and faster, she began falling slower and slower – until she was floating.

She landed gently, just in time to see the rabbit disappear through a tiny door. Alice was too big to follow him.

The Doorknob suggested she take a sip from a bottle on the table, which said "drink me" on the label. Alice drank and with every sip, she got smaller.

She tried to open the door, but now the Doorknob told her that he was locked. He suggested she try a biscuit from the box labelled "eat me." Alice did and she began to grow. Soon she was crying giant tears. She took another sip from the bottle and grew smaller and smaller until she could float through the keyhole.

On the other side of the door, Alice found herself in the strangest place. There were talking birds and walking fish, and a Cheshire cat who kept appearing and disappearing.

Alice kept hoping that one of these creatures could help her find the White Rabbit, but they were no help at all.

She came upon a pair of twins. They introduced

themselves as Tweedledum and Tweedledee.

"How do you do, Tweedledum and Tweedledee?" Alice greeted them. She could not tell them apart at all.

"When first meeting someone, you should shake hands and state your name and business," said Tweedledum, grabbing Alice's hand and shaking it firmly.

"That's manners!" said Tweedledee, grabbing her other hand and giving it a good squeeze.

With that, the twins danced Alice round and round. But they were so rough that they knocked her over! Alice was not pleased.

"Talk about manners!" She exclaimed, picking herself

up. "If you must know, my name is Alice, and I'm following the White Rabbit. I'm very sorry, but I must hurry."

Despite the twins'

protests, Alice went on her way. Soon she came to an unusual garden. Flying about were bread-and-butterflies and a rocking-horse fly. Alice discovered that the flowers in Wonderland could speak!

"What kind of flower are you?" a big orchid asked her.

"Oh, I'm not any kind of flower," Alice replied.

"No scent at all," added another flower, sniffing her. Alice did not know what to make of this.

"Just as I suspected!" a rose cried. "She's nothing but a common weed!" The rose turned her back on Alice.

"Leave!" shouted the flowers. "We don't want you in our lovely garden." They pointed to the way out.

Feeling very upset, Alice was forced to run away.

Then, nearby, Alice saw a familiar grin up in a tree. It was the Cheshire Cat. She asked if he'd seen the White Rabbit.

"No," replied the cat. "But if I were looking for him, I'd ask the Mad Hatter." And with that, the cat began to disappear, without telling her how to find him.

She walked a bit further, wondering what to do, until she came across two road signs pointing in the same direction. One read "Mad Hatter" and the other read "March Hare."

She followed the signs to a clearing in the woods where the Mad Hatter was giving a tea party with the March Hare. They made Alice feel quite unwelcome. They didn't offer her a cup of tea and wouldn't help her find the White Rabbit.

Alice went on her way and soon ran into the Cheshire Cat again. She explained that she was trying to find her way home. But the cat replied that all ways led to the Queen. He opened a door and Alice stepped through.

The White Rabbit hurried into view. He was about to announce the Queen! The Queen of Hearts arrived and invited Alice to play croquet. During their game, the Cheshire Cat appeared and tripped Her Majesty. The Queen was furious and blamed Alice. "Off with her head!" she cried. There was a mad chase and Alice ran through Wonderland to get away.

Suddenly Alice awoke on the riverbank.

"You've been dreaming," her sister said.

Alice looked around but didn't see any strange talking creatures. All she saw were her sister, the book, and Dinah, her kitten. And that was just fine with Alice.

WALT DISNEY'S

PeterPan

Long ago, in the city of London, there lived a family named Darling. Wendy, John, and Michael Darling would sit in the nursery telling stories about a far-off place called Never Land where the daring Peter Pan and the

pixie Tinker Bell lived.
And no one in Never
Land ever grew old.

Peter Pan and Tinker
Bell came to the Darlings'
nursery window one night
to look for Peter's lost
shadow. It wasn't Peter's
first visit to the Darling
house. He had come there

many times before to listen to Wendy's stories. Peter was

upset when Wendy explained how she was nearly grown up

now and that this was her last night in the nursery.

"But that means no more stories," cried Peter, "unless I take you all back to Never Land with me."

"That would be wonderful," the children shouted.

"But how will we get there?" Wendy asked.

"All you've got to do is fly," Peter replied.

With the help of a sprinkling of pixie dust from Tinker Bell, they took off and soared away towards Never Land.

After they had been flying for a while they saw amazing waterfalls. Mermaid Lagoon lay beneath them. There was a pirate ship, a forest, and an Indian camp too. It was the most beautiful place.

The pirate ship belonged to Captain Hook. The Captain

had two enemies in Never Land – Peter Pan and a hungry

crocodile. One day, during a fight, the crocodile had

managed to take a chunk from Hook's hand and had

followed him around ever since, hoping for the rest of him.

When they landed, Peter took Wendy, Michael, and John to meet his friends, the Lost Boys. Then he and Wendy went to the lagoon. There Peter spied the Indian Chief's daughter, Tiger Lily, tied up in Hook's boat.

They heard Hook ask Tiger Lily where Peter Pan's

hideout was, but the Indian princess wouldn't tell him.

"I have to save Tiger Lily!" Peter cried. He and Wendy

followed Hook to Skull Rock. Peter challenged the Captain

to a duel. Peter was too quick and too clever for Hook.

After a few minutes, the Captain was in the water with the

hungry crocodile!

Peter rescued Tiger Lily and brought her back to the Indian camp.

Captain Hook got away from the crocodile and swore revenge against Peter Pan. He kidnapped Tinker

Bell and tricked her into telling him where Peter lived.

The pirates went to Peter's hideout but he wasn't there.

They captured Wendy, John, Michael and the Lost Boys instead.

Knowing that Peter would return, they left him a beautifully wrapped package to find. As soon as he opened it, BOOM! It would explode. And that would be the end of Peter Pan.

Tinker Bell knew what Hook had planned. She had to warn Peter before it was too late! She made her escape and flew back to the hideout.

Meanwhile, on Hook's ship, Wendy was about to walk

the plank. "Peter Pan will save us," she insisted.

But the evil captain just laughed at her. "Pan will

never save you now!" he cried with glee.

Captain Hook didn't realise that Tinker Bell was

already on her way to find him.

Peter and Tinker Bell returned in a flash. "Hook, this time you've gone too far!" Peter shouted as he challenged him to one last duel.

Wendy, Michael, John, and the Lost Boys watched in awe as Peter fought bravely to save them. At last Hook and the pirates ended up in the water. They swam as fast as they could, with the always-hungry crocodile close behind.

"Thank you so much for saving us," said Wendy. "And now I think it's time for us to go back home."

Before they could say "Captain Hook," Peter had set sail in Hook's ship through the skies of Never Land.

They were soon all back in London safe and sound.

Peter and Tinker Bell said their good-byes, and the children promised never to forget the wonderful times they had had. As the years went by, they would remember everything – Peter, Tinker Bell, the Pirates, Tiger Lily, and the Lost Boys – just as if it had all happened yesterday.

WALT DISNEY'S

Lady and the TRAMP

Lady was a happy little dog. She lived in a big house with Jim Dear and Darling. One day Lady learned that Darling was expecting a baby. Lady didn't know that

things in the house would soon be very different.

One day Lady met a scruffy dog named Tramp. Tramp had no home and no family. He went wherever he pleased and did whatever he pleased.

"Believe me," Tramp told Lady and her friends Jock and Trusty, "babies change everything! Now you'll have nothing but trouble. Just wait and see!"

But Tramp was wrong. When the baby arrived, Lady had one more wonderful person to care for and love.

Several weeks later, Jim Dear and Darling went off on a trip. Aunt Sarah came to stay at the house. "Lady," said Jim Dear, "help Aunt Sarah take care of the baby."

Aunt Sarah brought her Siamese cats with her.

They made a lot of trouble.
Lady barked at the cats,
but it did no good.

"Shame on you, Lady!"
shouted Aunt Sarah.
"Attacking my poor little
angels. A muzzle is what
you need!" She took
Lady straight to the pet
shop to buy one.

The muzzle was more than Lady could bear, and she
ran away. After a while, she stopped to catch her breath,

and found herself in a strange part of town, surrounded by a pack of nasty looking dogs.

Just then her friend Tramp appeared. Seeing that Lady was in danger, he fought the stray dogs and chased them off.

"You poor thing!" said Tramp, looking at the muzzle. He took Lady to the zoo, where a friendly beaver chewed right through the muzzle and freed Lady.

Tramp took Lady to one of his favourite places. They shared a romantic dinner for two at Tony's Italian restaurant.

Finally, after a stroll through the park, Lady said, "I must go home. I have to take care of the baby."

"Okay," said Tramp. "But let's have a few laughs before you go!"

"Tramp, no!" said Lady. But Tramp had already rushed into a nearby farmyard to chase the squawking chickens.

Suddenly the dogcatcher appeared and captured them all, except Tramp who ran away. Lady was taken to the animal shelter. She was frightened – especially when the other dogs began to tease her. A dog named Peg came to

Lady's rescue. "Can't you see she's scared enough already?" Peg said to the other dogs.

The dogs were jealous because Lady had a shiny address disk around her neck which meant she'd be going home.

When Lady finally did go home, Tramp paid her a visit. "I'm sorry," he said sadly. Lady refused to speak to him.

That night, Lady saw a rat scurry up a tree by the

baby's room. She was tied up, so all she could do was bark.

When Tramp heard Lady barking, he came running.

"What's wrong?" he asked.

When Lady told him about the rat, Tramp ran into the

house and up the stairs.

Lady pulled at her chain until it broke. Then she ran to help Tramp fight the rat.

"You brutes!" cried Aunt Sarah when she saw Lady and Tramp in the baby's room. "Get away from the baby!" The room was a mess.

Aunt Sarah called the dogcatcher to come and take Tramp away.

When Jim Dear and Darling came home that night, Lady helped Jim Dear find the dead rat.

"Lady," said Jim Dear thankfully, "I think you and your friend were trying to save our baby from the rat."

Meanwhile, Jock and Trusty went to find Tramp. They soon caught up with the dogcatcher's wagon. Trusty

began barking very loudly – so loudly, in fact, that he

scared the horses. They reared up and the wagon tipped

over right onto poor Trusty.

Trusty had a broken leg, but he would be okay.

Lady and Jim Dear arrived just in time to free Tramp.

They were so grateful to him that they asked Tramp to live with them always.

By Christmas of that year, Lady and Tramp had four puppies – and the family's happiness was complete.

Walt Disney's Sleeping Beauty

Long ago, in a faraway kingdom, a tiny princess was born. Her parents, the King and Queen, named her Aurora. Her parents announced that Aurora would one day marry young Prince Phillip, who lived in a neighbouring kingdom.

To celebrate Aurora's birth, the King held a great feast at the castle. People came from near and far, bringing gifts for the child.

Three good fairies came too, and they brought the baby very special gifts.

"Mine shall be the gift of beauty," said the first good fairy. "Mine shall be the gift of song," said the second.

Before the third good fairy could speak, an evil witch named Maleficent appeared. She was angry because she hadn't been invited to the feast.

Maleficent warned that on Aurora's sixteenth birthday, the girl would prick her finger on a spinning wheel and die.

But the third good fairy had not yet spoken. "No, the Princess will not die!" she said quickly. "She will only sleep – until true love's kiss breaks the spell."

To keep Aurora safe, the King and Queen secretly sent her to live with the good fairies.

The fairies called the child Briar Rose so that no one would know who she was.

On the day of Briar Rose's sixteenth birthday, the fairies sent her to pick berries in the woods. Then they

began preparing for her birthday party.

The fairies had decided not to use magic for fear that they would be discovered by Maleficent. But after struggling with a lopsided cake and a dress that just didn't look right, they retrieved their magic wands and set about making everything perfect for Briar Rose.

Meanwhile, beautiful Briar Rose wandered through the woods with her animal friends. Suddenly a handsome young man appeared. Briar Rose did not know it was Prince Phillip.

Later that day, when the birthday celebration was over, the three fairies led the Princess back to the castle. She was going to live with her parents once again.

That night the evil fairy Maleficent appeared at the castle and lured Aurora away to a lonely tower. There she tricked the Princess into touching a spinning wheel. Aurora pricked her finger

and fell into a deep sleep.

To save the King and Queen from terrible heartache, the good fairies put everyone in the castle to sleep.

Meanwhile, Maleficent wanted to keep Prince Phillip away from Aurora, so she locked the Prince in a dungeon.

Phillip was not a prisoner for long. The good fairies brought him a magic shield and sword. Soon he was on his way to rescue the Princess.

To keep Prince Phillip from entering the castle, Maleficent surrounded it with thick branches full of

thorns. But that didn't stop the Prince. As he came closer to the castle, Maleficent turned herself into an angry dragon.

There was a terrible fight, but Phillip used his magic

shield and sword and finally defeated the dragon.

Prince Phillip raced to the tower and found the sleeping beauty. He kissed her tenderly, and the Princess awoke.

At the same moment, everyone in the castle awoke. The King and Queen were overjoyed to see their daughter again.

Soon it was announced that Princess Aurora and Prince Phillip would marry. Everyone in the kingdom rejoiced, for they knew that Aurora and her prince would live happily ever after.

WALT DISNEY'S
101 DALMATIANS

Pongo, Perdita, and their fifteen puppies lived in a cosy little house in London. The house belonged to their owners, Roger and Anita. They were perfectly happy until they met Cruella De Vil – Anita's old schoolfriend who simply loved spotted puppies.

She wanted to buy them all and make them into spotted fur coats!

Roger put his foot down. "These puppies are not for sale and that's final," he said.

Cruella was furious and refused to give up.

One night Cruella's two nasty henchmen, Horace and

Jasper, kidnapped the puppies! Then they drove out to Cruella's old country estate and waited to hear from their boss.

When the puppies got there, they saw lots and lots of other Dalmatian puppies who had also been snatched by Horace and Jasper.

Back at home, Pongo and Perdita could not believe what had happened.

Perdita knew at once that Cruella was behind her missing puppies.

"She has stolen them," sobbed Perdita. "Oh, Pongo, do you think we'll ever find them?"

Pongo knew the Twilight Bark was their only hope. He would bark his message to all the dogs in London.

They would pick it up and pass it along to the dogs in the country. And maybe someone would find the puppies.

That night Pongo's message reached a quiet farm where an old English sheepdog known as Colonel lay sleeping peacefully.

"Alert, alert!" shouted Sergeant Tibs, a cat who lived on the farm. "Vital message coming in from London."

The Colonel listened closely. "Fifteen puppies have been stolen!" he cried.

Sergeant Tibs remembered hearing barking at the old De Vil place. They headed straight for the gloomy mansion.

The Colonel helped Tibs look through the window. Sure enough, there were the fifteen puppies – plus their eighty-four new friends!

Tibs and the Colonel overheard Cruella, Jasper, and Horace talking. When they heard her plans to make coats out of the puppies, they knew there was no time to waste. The Colonel ran off to get word to Pongo and Perdita while Tibs helped the puppies escape!

As soon as Horace and Jasper realised what was

happening, they tried to stop the puppies. But it was too late. Pongo and Perdita arrived and fought off the foolish thugs as the puppies hurried to safety.

Once all the dogs were safely out of the house, they

thanked the Colonel and Tibs and went on their way. A

black Labrador arranged a lift to London for them in the

back of a van that was about to set off. The dogs waited

in a blacksmith's shop until the coast was clear.

Suddenly Cruella's big car drove up the street. She

had followed their tracks and was looking for them.

But Pongo had a clever idea. There were ashes in the

fireplace. If they all rolled in them, they would be disguised in black soot. Then they could jump aboard the van without Cruella realising it was them!

It worked perfectly until a lump of snow dripped onto a puppy and washed off a patch of soot. From her car, Cruella could see it was a Dalmatian puppy.

"They're escaping!" she cried as the van took off.

There was a terrible chase. Cruella tried to pass the van on the road, but she ended up crashing through a barricade and driving right into a huge pile of snow. Cruella's beautiful car was a wreck! And that wasn't all.

She had lost the puppies! Cruella threw a tantrum.

Pongo and Perdita and 99 puppies eventually arrived back home safely, much to Roger and Anita's delight. Roger pulled

out a handkerchief and wiped Pongo's face clean.

"What will we do with all these puppies?" Anita asked.

"We'll keep them," Roger answered. He sat down at the piano and composed a song right on the spot. "We'll buy a big place in the country, and we'll have a plantation," he sang. "A Dalmatian plantation!"

And that's exactly what they did.

Walt Disney's

The JungleBook

Long ago, deep in the jungles of faraway India, there lived a wise black panther named Bagheera. One day, as Bagheera sat in a tree, he saw something surprising. "Why, it's a Man-cub!" said the panther.

Bagheera was not able to care for the Man-cub, so he took the baby to live with a family of wolves.

The wolves named the little boy Mowgli and raised him as one of their own.

Ten rainy seasons came and went. Mowgli grew, and

no Man-cub was happier than he. The creatures of the

jungle were good to him.

But one jungle animal did not wish Mowgli well. It was Shere Khan, the strong and cunning tiger.

Shere Khan feared nothing but Man's gun and Man's fire. He was sure the Man-cub would grow up to be a hunter.

"Shere Khan has returned to our part of the jungle!" Akela the wolf said one day. "Surely

he will try to kill the boy." Mowgli was no longer safe.

"It is time for Mowgli to return to his own kind," Bagheera said. "I will take him to the Man village."

"Hurry," Akela said. "There is no time to lose."

Bagheera and Mowgli started on their way.

"We'll spend the night here," Bagheera said as they settled down on the branch of a tree.

Just then Kaa the snake appeared. He thought Mowgli would make a tasty morsel. The snake used his hypnotic eyes to put Mowgli in a trance. He wrapped the Man-cub in his coils.

Bagheera awoke just in time to smack Kaa on the head

and send him on his way. It was time to get going!

But Mowgli didn't want to go back to the man village. "The jungle is my home!" the Man-cub insisted. He went off on his own.

Along the way Mowgli saw a parade of elephants. He thought it was wonderful and wanted to march along with them. But when it came time for the elephant inspection, Colonel Hathi took a closer look at Mowgli.

"What happened to your trunk?" asked the Colonel, scooping him up and looking stern. "Why – you're a Man-cub!" he cried.

Bagheera came to Mowgli's rescue. He insisted on

taking him to the Man village, but Mowgli refused once more. "Then from now on, you're on your own!" Bagheera told him.

Mowgli soon met a good-natured bear named Baloo. Baloo helped Mowgli forget his troubles. They played together, swam together, and ate sweet, ripe bananas and coconuts all day long.

As the two friends floated on the river, a group of monkeys swooped down on Mowgli. They picked him up

and dragged him off to the
ancient city of the
monkey king.

The monkey king
wanted something
from Mowgli.
"Teach me the secret
of fire," King Louie
demanded. "Then
I can be human like you!"

Bagheera and Baloo arrived in time to help Mowgli
escape from the monkeys. "Now you see why you must

leave the jungle!" they pleaded.

But Mowgli still did not believe his friends. He ran away from them again – right into the great Shere Khan himself.

"I'm not afraid of you!" said Mowgli bravely.

A storm began to blow around them. Suddenly a bolt of lightning struck nearby.

The lightning started a small fire. Mowgli grabbed a burning branch and tied it to Shere Khan's tail. The terrified tiger ran away, never to be seen again.

As Mowgli proudly walked through the jungle with his friends, he heard a new and beautiful sound. It was a girl from the Man village, singing a sweet song.

He listened. "Go on, Mowgli!" Bagheera urged.

Mowgli knew that he must follow the girl. She smiled at him as he walked with her to the village.

Baloo and Bagheera watched Mowgli go. Their hearts were sad, but they knew it was as it should be. Their Man-cub had found his way home at last.

DISNEY'S
THE ARISTOCATS

Madame Bonfamille and her amazing Aristocats lived in a beautiful house in Paris. There were Marie, Toulouse, Berlioz, and Duchess, their mama. The kittens were very talented. Madame loved them very

much and planned to leave her entire fortune to them.

Madame did not keep this fact a secret, and her wishes did not make Edgar the butler very happy. Edgar came up with a plan. He would make the Aristocats disappear so he could inherit Madame's fortune!

For supper that very evening, Edgar prepared the cats a special dish. "Come and taste this delicious creme de la creme à la Edgar!" he called.

Unfortunately, it was very delicious. The Aristocats and their friend Roquefort the mouse gulped it all down. They soon fell fast asleep.

Edgar put them all in a basket and drove them out into the country in the sidecar of his motorcycle. He soon met two noisy dogs who loved to chase anything on wheels.

Edgar lost control of his motorcycle and drove straight into a river!

The basket holding the Aristocats fell off, and landed under the bridge. When the cats awoke, they did not

know where they were. How would they find their way home?

Soon Thomas O'Malley, the alley cat, found the Aristocats and offered his help. He was quite taken with Duchess. O'Malley arranged a ride aboard a milk truck. But the cats were discovered and chased off the truck.

Concerned for their safety, O'Malley decided to accompany the Aristocats back to Paris. After the very long walk, O'Malley convinced Duchess to stop at his house and rest before going home to Madame.

But when they got there, his jazz-playing friends were

singing and dancing up a storm. And the Aristocats wanted to meet them all, especially Scat Cat. The kittens joined in the fun, but soon it was time to go home. O'Malley tried to talk Duchess into staying with him, but she was too worried about Madame.

O'Malley agreed to take the Aristocats home.

He no sooner saw them to their door when Roquefort came running after him. "Duchess needs help!" cried the little mouse. "Come quickly!"

When Edgar had seen that the Aristocats were back, he'd grabbed them and stuffed them inside a pillowcase. Then he'd hidden them in the oven while he pulled out a huge trunk stamped "Timbuktu."

O'Malley sent Roquefort to get Scat Cat and his friends and bring them to Madame's house. Then he ran back to help Duchess. He managed to corner Edgar in the barn and there was a terrible fight.

Edgar pinned O'Malley to the wall with a pitchfork!

Suddenly Scat Cat and his friends were at the barn

door. They managed to overpower Edgar. As Roquefort

popped open the trunk to let the Aristocats out, the

animals made sure that Edgar took their place inside. A few minutes later, some men came to pick up the trunk headed for Timbuktu.

There was the happiest of reunions with Madame! She could not believe her precious cats were home safe and sound. And Madame had Thomas O'Malley and his friends to thank for it.

Madame could see that O'Malley and Duchess were in love. She invited him to live with them. Now her family was complete. And as for O'Malley's musician friends, Madame threw a great party and invited them all to play!

Disney's

MICKEY'S
CHRISTMAS CAROL

It was Christmas Eve. But old Ebenezer Scrooge didn't care. Poor Bob Cratchit, who worked for Scrooge, had to ask if he could have Christmas Day off. It took all of Cratchit's courage to face his mean boss.

"Christmas!" shouted the miserly Scrooge. "Bah, humbug!" But he gave his permission. Poor Cratchit hurried home

to his family before Scrooge could change his mind.

Just then, Scrooge's nephew Fred stopped by. "Come and join us for Christmas dinner, Uncle," he offered.

The old man just scowled. "Christmas! Bah, humbug!" was his only reply, as he shooed Fred out of the door.

After counting his money, Scrooge left for home. Sinking into his favourite chair after a bit of dinner,

Scrooge began to doze off. Suddenly, he sat up with a start!

CLINK-CLANK-CLINK! The ghost of Jacob Marley, Scrooge's dead business partner, was walking toward him in chains, moaning and groaning.

"I was selfish," said the ghost. "As I carry these chains through eternity, so will you, Scrooge!"

"No!" Scrooge cried. "I must be dreaming. It can't be.

Help me, Jacob. Tell me what I must do!"

"Tonight," Marley said, "three spirits will visit you. Listen to them and do as they say."

When the ghost disappeared, Scrooge shook his head. I need sleep, he thought. Perhaps it was a bit of indigestion.

He had just fallen asleep when the alarm clock rang. There on his bedside table stood a little

fellow. "I am the Ghost of Christmas Past," he said. The ghost held out his hand. "I'll take you to a Christmas of long ago." Scrooge and the spirit flew through the air.

They stopped at a house filled with music and laughter and people. There was a party going on.

"Why, that's me, when I was young!" Scrooge sighed.

"There's old Fezziwig. He gave me my first job. And there's my lovely Isabel."

The spirit reminded Scrooge that gold had taken the place of love in his heart. Scrooge turned away. "I don't want to see any more. Please, Spirit, take me home."

Suddenly the alarm rang once more. "I must have been dreaming again," Scrooge said, rubbing his eyes.

"Fee, fi, fo, fum!" yelled a voice. There sat a giant,

surrounded by a huge feast.

"What's all this?" Scrooge demanded.

"It's the food of generosity," the giant explained. "And

that's something you know nothing about! I'm the Ghost of Christmas Present. Come! See what's happening tonight." Scrooge followed the ghost to a tiny house.

He looked through the cracked window. It was Bob Cratchit's place.

"What a poor dinner they're having," Scrooge said sadly.

Then he asked, "What's wrong with the little lad?"

"Tiny Tim is very ill," said the giant. "He needs good food to make him strong and well. Pay his father more so he can buy his family enough to eat . . ." The giant's voice faded, and then he was gone.

Suddenly Scrooge heard another voice behind him. "I am the Ghost of Christmas Yet to Come," it said.

Scrooge turned to find himself in a graveyard. "Whose lonely grave is this?" he asked meekly.

"It belongs to a very rich man," the ghost said. "A man who was so selfish and unkind that he had no friends." The ghost waited for Scrooge's reaction.

Then Scrooge read the name on the stone. He couldn't believe his eyes! It was his very own grave!

"Oh, give me another chance!" cried Scrooge. "Tell me it's not too late to change my ways."

Scrooge kept pleading with the spirit until he woke up. There he was, alive and well and right in his own bed! Scrooge leaped out of bed with joy. It wasn't too late – he hadn't missed Christmas, after all. There was time to make up for his past mistakes.

He dressed quickly and rushed outside. First he tossed bags of money to the men collecting for the poor. Then he promised his nephew he would come for Christmas dinner after all. Now he just had one more visit to make.

Scrooge hurried over to Bob Cratchit's house.

He brought toys for Tiny Tim and the other children and

a wonderful Christmas dinner for everyone.

Cratchit and his wife were never more surprised or

pleased than by Scrooge's change of heart. Scrooge made

a promise to this family that from this day on they would never want for anything. What a Christmas miracle for the Cratchits and for Ebenezer Scrooge!

Tiny Tim had just one thing to say. "God bless us, every one!"

Disney's

OLIVER

& Company

Once upon a time, a little kitten lived on the busy streets of a big city. He was looking for a home. He met a street-smart dog named Dodger, who wanted his help stealing some food. The hungry kitten agreed to help out, in return for some sausages, but Dodger tricked him and ran off with their meal.

Disappointed and hungry, the kitten followed Dodger to a broken-down boat on the river. There he saw Dodger's  gang – Tito the Chihuahua, Francis the Bulldog, Einstein the Great Dane, and a lovely hound named Rita. Dodger was busy acting out the day's events and showing off the sausages they were about to have for dinner.

Suddenly there was a loud crash. The little kitten had fallen right through the roof!

The gang laughed and welcomed the kitten to their home. Soon their master, Fagin, walked in the door. Fagin wanted to see what his gang had collected that day. There was nothing but junk in the box. A car horn sounded outside, making Fagin jump.

"Yikes! It's Sykes," he said worriedly.

Fagin owed Sykes money and did not have a way to repay him. And Sykes was mean. While Fagin begged for more time, Sykes's Dobermans came aboard the barge and began pushing everybody around. When they tried to corner the kitten, he reached out and scratched one of the Dobermans on the nose.

Fagin and his gang were very impressed with the kitten's bravery, and decided to make him one of the gang.

At least the kitten had a home for now.

The next day the gang went out to find money for

Fagin. Tito saw a Limousine and wanted to check it out.

He took the kitten with him. But when Tito accidentally

set off the car alarm, the gang fled, leaving the poor kitten tangled up inside.

The little kitten didn't know that there was a passenger in the back seat – a little girl named Jenny. She scooped up the kitten and told Winston, the driver, to take them home. She wanted to give the kitten something to eat.

At home, Jenny's pampered poodle, Georgette,

resented the little kitten. But Jenny fell in love with him and named him Oliver. She even got him a special collar and name tag.

Soon Dodger and the gang turned up at the house to rescue Oliver. But Oliver didn't want to leave. He belonged with Jenny now. The gang didn't know how Oliver felt. They thought they were helping him. When they got him back to Fagin's,

the dogs realised they had made a mistake.

Fagin saw Oliver's smart new collar and new Fifth Avenue address. To Fagin, Fifth Avenue meant lots of money. This was his way out with Sykes! He would contact the owner at Fifth Avenue, tell them that he had found their cat, and ask for a reward. Then he could pay Sykes back. He organised the handover but was shocked

when Jenny appeared to get Oliver. He couldn't take money from such a little girl.

When Sykes drew up to collect his money, he saw Fagin was letting the little girl go. He was furious, grabbed Jenny and kidnapped her. "I'm sure someone will pay a nice ransom for you," Sykes said as he sped away.

Fagin and his gang were determined to help Oliver and Georgette find Jenny. They hopped onto Fagin's scooter and followed the car to Sykes's warehouse. The dogs made their way inside, where they found Jenny tied up. They were just about to rescue her when Sykes and his Dobermans found them.

Suddenly Fagin drove his scooter into the warehouse, and they all jumped on. Sykes followed them. The chase was on! Fagin headed for the

railway bridge, sure that Sykes couldn't follow him in his car. But he did!

Fagin drove his scooter onto the train tracks with Sykes close behind.

Oliver suddenly jumped into the car to make sure Jenny was okay, and bit Sykes's hand. The gang

managed to grab
Jenny and then, just
as one of Sykes's dogs
was about to get
Oliver, he jumped
out through the
sunroof.

A train was coming! Fagin managed to steer onto

another track, but Sykes's car crashed into the train.

Jenny didn't know what had happened to Oliver. She

was terribly worried. Just then Dodger walked up to her

carrying the little kitten by his neck. When Oliver saw

Jenny, he began to purr. Jenny was overjoyed that Oliver was all right.

The very next day was Jenny's birthday. She had a big party at her house. Fagin and the gang were all there. Everyone was happy. But nobody was happier than the little orphan kitten who had finally found a home.

Disney's

THE PRINCE AND THE PAUPER

Once upon a time there was a good and kindly king. He ruled his country with fairness and generosity. But one day the King became very ill and could no longer watch over his kingdom. His son, the Prince, stayed by his father's bedside, worrying.

The greedy captain of the guards saw this as his chance to rob the King's loyal subjects, since the King was too ill to protect them. Day after day, the Captain and his soldiers filled up the

palace with mountains of gold. Nobody could save the kingdom from the thieving man, until . . .

Two peasants wandered near the palace looking for food. One of the paupers, Mickey, looked exactly like the

Prince. Of course, he didn't have fine clothes to wear or live in a palace, but he did have two loyal friends. One was a rather silly fellow called Goofy, and the other was a friendly dog named Pluto.

Mickey and Goofy watched as the Captain of the Guards sped by in a royal coach filled with food. Pluto was so hungry that he chased the coach to the palace.

"Stop!" Mickey shouted. "Come back!" And he ran off after his dog.

When Mickey got to the palace, a guard waved him in and called him "Your Majesty."

Meanwhile, inside the palace, the real prince was sitting through another boring lesson with Professor Horace. To amuse himself, he took out his peashooter and aimed it at his servant, Donald.

A little later,

there was a loud crash in the hallway. The Prince and the pauper had each hidden in a suit of armour. When they went tottering down the hallway, they crashed into each other. Lifting their helmets, the two stared and stared.

The Prince talked Mickey into changing places, and headed out of the palace.

The Prince made it past the royal guard, but he couldn't fool Mickey's dog Pluto.

When Goofy saw the Prince, he was sure it was Mickey and struck up a conversation. The Prince said hello but then ran off.

Back at the palace, Donald brought food to Mickey's room. Mickey reached out for a turkey leg, but Donald grabbed it first.

"I'm checking it for poison," he said, biting into a juicy drumstick.

Pretty soon Donald had eaten all the food. Poor

Mickey didn't even get a bite.

Next it was time for the royal lessons. Mickey did

not fare very well at falconry or horse-riding. But the

Prince wasn't doing any better. He had tried to go

sledging with Mickey's friends.

The Prince headed for the marketplace, where he saw the Captain of the Guards stealing food from the poor people. He ordered the Captain to stop, but the Captain just looked at the raggedy peasant and laughed.

A few minutes later, the town crier came through the

square with news that the King had died.

"I must go back to the palace straight away," the Prince said. "I will miss my father greatly, but now it is my duty to take over as king."

"Gosh," said Goofy. "You're the Prince? I thought you

were my friend Mickey."

"I am your friend from now on," vowed the Prince, rushing off to the palace.

The Captain of the Guards was waiting for His Royal Highness.

As soon as the Prince got back to the palace, he was thrown into the dungeon.

"I see your royal ring," the Captain said. "But it won't

do you any good. As soon as the pauper is crowned king, I shall unmask him as an impostor and rule the kingdom myself!"

But the Prince was not alone in the dungeon. Donald was there, too!

Soon a strange-looking guard came to unlock the dungeon door. It was Goofy! He let the Prince out just in time for the coronation.

Meanwhile, Mickey was stalling and trying to avoid being crowned king. "Please don't put it on my head!" he begged.

"He is not the Prince!" yelled the wicked captain. "He's an impostor! Seize him!"

"But *I'm* not an impostor!" came a voice from a high balcony. It was the real prince! There was a

huge fight and Mickey, the Prince, and their friends trapped the Captain of the Guards and his soldiers.

Finally the Prince was crowned king. His first act was to arrest the Captain and his men.

Now that the kingdom was once again in kind, caring hands, Mickey was happily reunited with his friends and faithful dog. And the new king was content.

DISNEY'S
THE LITTLE
MERMAID

Once upon a time there was a little mermaid named Ariel who lived in a kingdom under the sea.

Every day Ariel longed for the world above the ocean. "If only I could be a human instead of a mermaid," she said to herself.

Ariel's father, King Triton, found out that Ariel had
been swimming to the ocean's surface even though it was
forbidden.

"Keep an eye on Ariel," the king ordered Sebastian the
crab. "Don't let
her go near any
humans!"

But Sebastian
could not stop Ariel.
One day she
approached a sailing
ship where she

spied a handsome
prince named Eric.

Suddenly a terrible
storm came up. Ariel
saw Prince Eric fall
overboard.

"I've got to save
him!" she cried. She

found the Prince and pulled him to safety, just alive.

Before Eric awoke, Ariel sang to him. She thought he
was the most wonderful human she'd ever seen.

Long after Ariel returned to the sea, Eric could hear

her beautiful voice in his dreams.

King Triton found out that Ariel had disobeyed him once again. "I told you to stay away from humans!" he shouted.

"But, Daddy, I love him!" Ariel cried. She had to see Prince Eric again.

Later that day, Ariel went to Ursula, the evil sea witch. Ursula promised to turn Ariel into a human – for a price. "You must give me your voice," Ursula commanded. "And if your prince doesn't kiss you in three days, you're mine!"

Ariel agreed to give Ursula her voice. Within seconds,

she had human legs and could no longer swim. Sebastian
and Flounder had to help her to shore.

When the Prince found Ariel, he did not know who
she was. "Can't you speak?" he asked. "Then let me help

you. I'll take you to my palace."

On the second day of Ariel's visit, Prince Eric took her on a tour of his kingdom. They went for a romantic boat ride in the lagoon. But before Eric could kiss her, Ursula's nasty eels overturned the boat.

Ursula knew she needed to take matters into her own tentacles. So she changed herself into a beautiful girl named Vanessa. Ariel's voice was tucked safely inside a shell around Vanessa's neck.

As soon as Eric heard the voice, he became hypnotized. He agreed to marry Vanessa that very day aboard his ship.

Ariel's friend Scuttle the seagull discovered Ursula's trick. He led an army of birds and sea creatures to the ship, hoping to stop the wedding.

In the struggle that followed, Vanessa's necklace

shattered. Instantly, Eric awoke from his trance and Ariel

got her voice back. Now she could finally tell Eric who

she really was.

But just then, the sun set, and Ariel was turned back

into a mermaid. The sea witch grabbed her and dived overboard. Eric followed them into the sea. He fought Ursula with all his strength and wits, and finally destroyed her.

At last, Ariel was back with her father under the sea.

But she was very unhappy. Now she and her prince

would never be together.

Even King Triton could see how unhappy Ariel was.

"I think she really loves him," the King said to Sebastian.

Sebastian nodded, and Triton knew what he must do.

The King waved his trident, making Ariel human again. Soon, aboard the royal ship, Ariel said good-bye to her friends under the sea. She and her prince were together forever. The Little Mermaid's wish had finally come true.

Disney's

Beauty _and the_ Beast

Once upon a time there was a prince who was so selfish and unkind that he and all who lived in his castle were put under a powerful spell.

The prince was turned into a terrible beast. He would

change back into a prince only if he learned to love someone and be loved in return.

In a nearby village lived a beautiful young woman named Belle. She loved to read books about adventure and romance.

Gaston, the hunter, followed Belle everywhere in town. He wanted to marry her, but Belle thought Gaston was a conceited bully.

One dark winter day, Belle's father, Maurice, started off on a journey through the woods and lost his way. Maurice found shelter in the Beast's gloomy castle. There he was greeted by the servants. The spell had changed them all into enchanted objects.

Before long Maurice was discovered by the enormous and frightening Beast!

"What are you staring at?" roared the angry Beast.

Then he threw Maurice into a dungeon.

Maurice's horse came home alone. "Where's Papa?" cried Belle. "Take me to him!" Belle climbed on, and the horse galloped back to the Beast's castle.

The Beast terrified Belle, but she tried to be brave.

"Let my father go!" she cried. "Let me take his place."

The Beast agreed, but only if Belle promised to stay in his gloomy castle forever.

The Beast's enchanted servants welcomed Belle and

tried to make her feel at home. There was Cogsworth the

clock, Lumiere the candelabra, and Mrs Potts the teapot.

They knew that if Belle and the Beast fell in love, the

spell that lay over the castle would be broken.

Little by little the Beast grew kinder toward Belle.

One day he led her to his magnificent library.

"It's wonderful!" Belle gasped.

"It's yours," said the Beast.

Belle slowly grew fonder of the Beast and learned to trust him. She even taught him how to dance. But her heart ached for her father. "If only I could see him again," she told the Beast.

"Come with me," he answered. "I will show him to you."

The Beast handed her a magic mirror. Belle held it up and saw her father looking tired and sick.

"I must go to him!" cried Belle.

The Beast agreed to let Belle go, even though it meant the end of his hopes for breaking the spell.

When Belle returned home, she told Gaston about the
Beast's kindness. Gaston was jealous.

He convinced the villagers that the Beast should be
destroyed, and led an angry mob to the castle.

Gaston found the Beast and fought him on the castle

rooftops. In the
midst of the battle,
Gaston lost his
footing and fell to
his death – but not
before he had
stabbed the Beast.

Belle rushed to the Beast's side only to find him badly wounded. "You came back," he whispered.

Belle's tears fell upon the Beast. "I love you," she cried. The spell was broken!

The Beast was transformed into a handsome prince, and the enchanted servants became human once more. Belle and her prince lived very happily ever after in their castle home.

Disney's

Aladdin

Long ago, in a faraway land called Agrabah, there lived a poor orphan named Aladdin. One day in the market, Aladdin stole some bread for his supper. The Sultan's guards chased him, but Aladdin and his pet monkey, Abu, escaped. Then Aladdin saw two hungry

children and gave the bread to them. "Things will change," he promised Abu. "Someday we'll live in a palace!"

That afternoon at the palace, Princess Jasmine was told by her father, the Sultan, that she must marry a prince in three days. Jasmine was very unhappy. "I will marry only for love!" she cried.

Jasmine told Rajah, her pet tiger, that she would have to leave the palace.

Disguising herself in an old peasant robe, the Princess ran away. Tired and hungry, Jasmine took an apple from a stall in the market, but couldn't pay the angry fruit seller. Aladdin came to her rescue. The mean merchant called the guards. They released the Princess, but took Aladdin to the palace dungeon.

Meanwhile, Jafar, the Sultan's evil advisor, disguised himself as a prisoner. "Help me find a very special lamp," he said to Aladdin, "and I'll set you free."

Jafar took Aladdin and Abu to the Cave of Wonders. A magic carpet appeared and led Aladdin to the lamp. But just as Aladdin reached for it, Abu grabbed a large, sparkling jewel.

The cave began to collapse. The magic carpet saved Aladdin and Abu, but all three were

trapped. "What's so special about this old lamp?" Aladdin

wondered aloud. As Aladdin rubbed the dusty lamp, an

enormous genie appeared.

"Master," he said, "I can grant you three wishes, but

you can't wish for more wishes. Now let's get out of here!"

Aladdin's first wish was to become a prince so Jasmine would want to marry him. He only had one wish left because he promised to save his last wish to set the Genie free.

Later that day, Aladdin arrived at the palace in grand style, introducing himself as Prince Ali Ababwa. Later that

evening Prince Ali took Jasmine for a ride on his magic carpet. The Prince looked very familiar. "Aren't you the boy from the marketplace?" asked Jasmine.

"No, I'm Prince Ali," Aladdin insisted, even though he knew he wasn't being honest.

The magic carpet took them back to the palace.

"That was wonderful," sighed Jasmine. She had fallen in love.

Aladdin was thrilled that things finally seemed to be going his way.

But suddenly the Sultan's guards, under orders from Jafar, appeared and grabbed poor Aladdin. After they tossed him into the sea, Aladdin summoned the Genie and used his second wish

to save his own life.

Aladdin returned to the palace with the lamp, but Iago, Jafar's parrot, stole it, and Jafar became the Genie's master.

"Make me Sultan," Jafar commanded.

"And make the Princess and her father my slaves."

The Genie was forced to obey. The poor sultan could only watch in horror as evil Jafar took over his kingdom.

He also had to watch his beautiful daughter wait on Jafar's every whim.

Jafar used his second wish to become an all-powerful sorcerer. He changed Aladdin back into a beggar and sent him far away. Aladdin thought he was doomed until the magic carpet appeared and helped him return to the palace. Jafar was furious, but Aladdin found a way to trick him.

"The Genie still has more power than you'll ever have," he told Jafar.

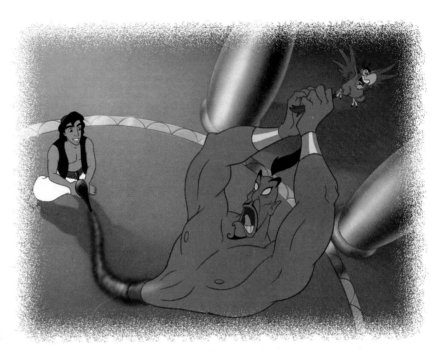

This infuriated Jafar and he used his third wish to become a genie. But he forgot one important thing. Genies become the prisoners of their lamps, shackled to them for all time. Jafar disappeared into a glowing black lamp.

To Jasmine's delight, the Sultan decided to let the

Princess choose her own husband. And there was only one choice for Jasmine – Aladdin.

Now it was Aladdin's turn to make someone happy. He turned to the Genie and said, "I wish for your freedom." And that was the best wish of all!

DISNEY'S
THE
LION KING

Everything in the animal kingdom had its place in the circle of life. When the Lion King, Mufasa, and his queen, Sarabi, had a cub named Simba, Mufasa knew that one day Simba would be king. Everyone bowed in respect as Rafiki the baboon introduced the young prince to all the animals.

Only one lion – Mufasa's brother, Scar – refused to attend the ceremony. He was not happy that Simba would be next in line for Mufasa's throne instead of him.

Simba grew into a happy, healthy cub. One day he proudly told his uncle Scar, "One day I'm going to rule the whole kingdom! Everything except that shadowy place.

I'm not allowed to go there."

"You're absolutely right, Simba," his uncle agreed slyly. "Only the bravest lions can go to the elephant graveyard." Scar deliberately tempted his adventurous nephew.

Simba raced home and convinced his friend Nala to explore the elephant graveyard with him.

It was more frightening than they had ever imagined.

Zazu, Mufasa's advisor, caught up with the cubs and warned them it was too dangerous to carry on.

But Simba only laughed at Zazu. Then he heard someone laughing back. He turned to see three enemy hyenas ready for lunch. "He's a king fit for a meal," laughed one.

The nasty hyenas

chased the cubs right into a trap. Suddenly there was a

tremendous roar. Mufasa arrived and frightened the

hyenas away.

Simba was very proud of his father. "We'll always be

together, won't we?"

he asked Mufasa

later that evening.

"Look up at the

stars, Simba," said

Mufasa. "Those are

the great kings of

the past looking

down on us.
Remember those
kings will always be
there to guide you,
and so will I."

Although Scar was
very angry with the
hyenas for letting
Simba escape, he made a bargain with them. If they
helped him become king, they could have their run of the
Pride Lands. And Scar had a plan.

Later Scar took Simba to a deep gorge and promised

him a wonderful surprise if he waited on a certain rock.

Then he signalled the hyenas.

The surprise was a stampeding herd of wildebeest!

The earth trembled as the wildebeest headed into the

gorge and straight towards Simba. Simba held onto a

branch but was

slipping fast.

In an instant

Mufasa appeared

and grabbed his

son. He carried

Simba to safety, but

then slipped off the ledge and fell into the thundering stampede.

When everything was quiet once more, Simba found his father lying lifeless at the foot of a cliff. Simba had not seen Scar push Mufasa to his death. Simba believed it was all his fault.

"Run away, Simba," Scar advised the young cub. "Run away and never return."

Scar watched as the young cub ran away, chased by

the hyenas. Scar returned to Pride Rock and announced to the lions that he would be their new king.

Simba ended up in the desert, where he collapsed from heat and exhaustion. Luckily two curious creatures found him – a meerkat called Timon and a warthog named Pumbaa.

Simba's new friends took him home to the jungle, where they introduced him to Timon's idea of hakuna matata – "no worries."

Simba tried to put the past behind him, but it was difficult. One day a young lioness appeared, looking for help. It was his old friend, Nala. She told Simba the sad story of how bad things were since Scar had taken over the Pride Lands.

But Simba could not face going back – until Rafiki appeared and led him to a vision of his dead father. "You are my son and the one true king. You must take your place in the circle of life," Mufasa explained.

So Simba returned to the Pride Lands with his friends by his side. There was a great battle. Scar cornered Simba

and confessed what he had done many years ago. "You didn't kill your father," Scar whispered menacingly. "I did."

At last Simba found the strength to fight back. He pushed the evil lion off the rock and into the jaws of the waiting hyenas.

When the fighting was over, Simba took his rightful place as king and restored the Pride Lands to a place of peace. And when Simba and Nala's little cub was born, a brand-new circle of life was begun.

DISNEY'S

POCAHONTAS

One day Pocahontas visited Grandmother Willow, a wise old tree spirit. Pocahontas was confused. Her father wanted her to marry Kocoum, a brave warrior. But Pocahontas did not believe this was the right path for her. She had dreamed of a spinning arrow and asked Grandmother Willow about the meaning of her dream.

"It is pointing you down your path," she told Pocahontas.

"But how do I find my path?" Pocahontas asked.

"Listen with your heart and you will understand," Grandmother Willow told her. "The spirits are everywhere. They will guide you."

So Pocahontas climbed a tall tree to listen to the wind. Off in the distance she saw strange, billowing clouds.

The clouds Pocahontas thought she saw were really the sails of a large ship. Aboard were men from England coming to the New World in search of gold.

When the ship came into shore, a man called John Smith set out to explore the new land. He met a funny raccoon called Meeko, Pocahontas's friend.

Pocahontas hid from the stranger. But when he heard rustling in the bushes, he knew someone was there. Finally the two stood face-to-face. Pocahontas

was scared; she ran to her canoe to get away. But the stranger called after her. "Don't go! I won't hurt you!"

Pocahontas did not understand what John Smith was saying, but she remembered Grandmother Willow's words. When she listened with her heart, she saw that he was kind. The two quickly became friends.

Meanwhile, at Governor Ratcliffe's orders, John

Smith's crew began digging up the new land in search of

gold. When the Indians from Pocahontas's tribe

approached the settlers, the Governor called them

"savages." He ordered his men to draw their guns and fire.

The Indians had never seen weapons like guns before. Powhatan, who was the chief and Pocahontas's father, declared war against these dangerous men.

Back in the forest, Pocahontas and John Smith gradually got to know each other. Ever curious, and always in search of food, Meeko took a compass from

John Smith's bag. "What is that?" Pocahontas asked.

"It helps you find your way when you're lost," John Smith explained. "Meeko can keep it. I can buy another one in London."

Pocahontas wanted to hear all about London. John

Smith described the wonders of the city. Then he told Pocahontas that the settlers would build a city like London in the New World. Pocahontas didn't think they needed a city in the middle of her beautiful forest. She decided it was time to introduce John Smith to the wonders of nature all around them.

Pocahontas even took John Smith to meet Grandmother Willow. He was amazed. "One look at this place and the men will forget about digging for gold," Smith said.

"What is gold?" Pocahontas asked.

John Smith showed her a gold coin. Pocahontas told him that there was nothing like this on her land.

John Smith rushed to his camp to tell Ratcliffe that there was no gold to be found. But the Governor didn't believe him. He thought the Indians wanted to keep it themselves. Ratcliffe wanted to take it by force.

When Pocahontas tried to tell her father that they must find a peaceful way to deal with the strangers, Powhatan's braves didn't agree. They wanted to fight. Pocahontas convinced her father that if one of the strangers would come and talk in peace, he must listen.

That night, Pocahontas met John Smith at the magical willow tree. She convinced him to talk to her father. But neither she nor John Smith knew that a settler named Thomas was watching them. So was Kocoum. Suddenly Kocoum jumped out of the woods and attacked John Smith. Thomas fired at Kocoum.

"Thomas, run!" Smith cried.

As Thomas fled, warriors captured Smith.

"At sunrise, this man will die," the chief told his people.

Pocahontas did not know what to do. Suddenly Meeko dropped the compass into her lap. She looked at the needle moving back and forth. "The spinning arrow!" she whispered.

"It's the arrow from your dream showing you your path. Let the spirits guide you," Grandmother Willow said.

Pocahontas ran like the wind. She stopped the

warriors from hurting Smith. The Indians put down their weapons and refused to fight.

But Ratcliffe grabbed a musket and shot at Powhatan. John Smith jumped in front of the chief and took the bullet himself.

The wounded Smith had to return to England. So did the greedy governor, who was now in chains.

As they were about to set sail, Pocahontas and her friend said good-bye. "Come with me?" John Smith asked hopefully.

"I am needed here," Pocahontas replied sadly.

"Then know that wherever I am, I'll always be with you." John Smith smiled as he left.

Pocahontas knew that in their hearts, they would always be together.

DISNEY'S
THE HUNCHBACK OF NOTRE DAME

Long, long ago in the city of Paris, a young, strange-looking man lived in the bell tower of the great Cathedral of Notre Dame. He was the bell ringer, Quasimodo. His name meant "half-formed," and had been

given to him by his cruel master, Judge Claude Frollo. Quasimodo's only friends were the stone gargoyles that decorated the cathedral.

Quasimodo longed to walk in the city below his tower prison, but Frollo forbade it. He was a mean man who hated everything and everyone – especially gypsies. He had even

convinced gentle Quasimodo that he was a monster, and

that terrible things would happen if he went out among

the people.

Once a year, all of Paris prepared for a great festival.

On that day, known as the Festival of Fools, the people

paraded around the city dressed in masks, hoping to be crowned the King of Fools. The gargoyles told Quasimodo that this year he must attend the festival.

Everyone was so busy having fun that no one noticed the poor bell ringer wandering around. He met the dancing gypsy, Esmeralda, and thought she was beautiful. So did

Phoebus, Frollo's new Captain of the Guard, who rode into Paris that same day.

When Quasimodo was crowned King of Fools, the people laughed. They threw ropes over him to hold him down. Frollo would not rescue Quasimodo, but Esmeralda ran to cut Quasimodo free.

Frollo was enraged. He ordered Phoebus to arrest her.

But Esmeralda and her grey goat, Djali, ran into the cathedral where she knew she would be safe. Frollo's soldiers could not touch her once she was inside. But Frollo warned her, "Set one foot

outside these walls, and you're my prisoner!"

Quasimodo did not understand. He believed that all

gypsies were bad, but Esméralda was good and kind and gentle. His master had been wrong. Maybe Frollo had been wrong about him, too. Maybe he wasn't a monster!

Quasimodo decided to help Esmeralda escape.

He carried her and Djali down the side of the cathedral. When they got to the street, she gave him a special amulet to keep. "Use this if you ever need help," she explained.

"It will lead you to the Court of Miracles, where you can find me." Then, promising to visit him soon, Esmeralda vanished.

Meanwhile, Phoebus convinced Esmeralda that he

was on her side – not Frollo's. When Phoebus refused to do the judge's bidding, Frollo turned on the Captain and ordered his soldiers to kill him. The injured Phoebus managed to escape with Esmeralda's

help. She took him to Quasimodo in the bell tower and asked him to hide Phoebus for her.

Quasimodo sadly agreed, for he could see that the two

were in love. Soon Frollo came to the bell tower, hoping

to trick Quasimodo into telling him where Esmeralda was

hiding. He convinced Quasimodo that he already knew

about the gypsies'

hideout, the Court of

Miracles, and planned

to attack at dawn.

Quasimodo and

Phoebus set out to

warn Esmeralda

about Frollo's plans.

Using the amulet,

they found their way to the Court of Miracles. They
did not realise something very important: They were
leading Frollo and his soldiers there, as well.

"Take them
away!" Frollo cried.
They were all his
prisoners now.

But chains could
not hold the
determined bell
ringer. Quasimodo
escaped and rescued

Esmeralda. Phoebus, the gypsies, Quasimodo, and the

gargoyles fought bravely against Frollo and his soldiers.

When the battle was over, the trio walked out of the

cathedral and into the sunlight smiling. Quasimodo was cheered by the crowd. The bell ringer who once thought he was a monster was now a great hero!

Walt Disney's

MICKEY
and the
BEANSTALK

Long, long ago, there was a place where the sun smiled all day. It was called Happy Valley. Everything in Happy Valley was pretty and green and . . . happy. The people who lived there were happy, too.

High on a hilltop overlooking this sweet little place stood a beautiful castle. In the castle lived a golden harp

who sang the day away. The harp had Happy Valley under her very happy spell.

Then one day a terribly sad thing

happened. Someone stole the golden harp from the castle
and broke the magic spell. Everything stopped working and
growing. And everyone stopped feeling happy. Soon there
was nothing to eat, and the people grew sad and hungry.

Three farmers decided there was nothing left to do but
sell their cow. Mickey took her into town. When he

returned, he showed Donald and Goofy the three beans he'd got for her.

"Three beans!" cried his friends. "We can't live on three beans!" Donald grabbed the beans and threw them on the floor.

"But . . . but . . . they are magic beans," Mickey tried to explain as he watched the beans roll through a crack in the floor, lost forever.

During the night, in bright moonlight, the beans began

to grow. They grew into a huge stalk that climbed all the way to the sky, carrying the farmers' little house with it.

When the hungry farmers awoke, they looked out of the window. Happy Valley was gone. All they could see from the beanstalk was a very big castle and a lot of fluffy clouds.

"Let's go and look!" cried Mickey. "Whoever lives in that

big castle must have plenty of food. Maybe he'll share it with us!"

Sure enough, when they crept inside the castle, they saw huge plates filled with delicious food. They helped themselves and as they finished eating, they heard a tiny voice call out to them from a box on the table.

"Who are you?" Mickey, Donald, and Goofy asked.

"It is I, the golden harp," said the tiny voice. "A giant stole me and brought me here to sing for him."

The farmers were very frightened when the heard the word "giant." They almost ran away, but Mickey told them that they couldn't leave without the magic harp.

"We have to rescue her and save Happy Valley!" he said.

Just then the room started shaking. Somebody as big as a giant was coming!

Mickey, Donald, and
Goofy ran and hid.

The giant walked
over to the table and
made himself a
sandwich. He was just
about to take a bite

when he noticed Mickey.

"Run!" Mickey shouted to Donald and Goofy.

The giant was very angry. He chased them around the

room until he had two of them cornered. Then he put

Donald and Goofy into the box with the golden harp,

locked it, and slipped the key into his pocket.

Mickey hid quietly until the giant fell asleep. Then he tiptoed over to the box and knocked.

"Get the key out of his pocket," the golden harp whispered.

Very carefully, Mickey took the key. The giant stirred

in his sleep, but he didn't wake up.

Mickey let his friends and the harp out of the box. Quietly, they made their way to the front door of the castle. But just as they were creeping past the giant, he opened one eye and saw them! What a roar he made!

Mickey decided to distract the giant so his friends could get the harp to safety. He teased the giant, who chased him all over the castle. Finally Mickey jumped out of an open window, ran over to the beanstalk, and slid down after his friends.

At the bottom, Donald and Goofy grabbed a saw and began to cut down the beanstalk as fast as they could. The giant kept climbing down, down, down. When the beanstalk fell, he crashed right through the ground with a mighty BANG!

The farmers took the golden harp back to her castle on the hilltop, where she could sing once more. And Happy Valley was once again a very happy place.

Walt Disney's

THREE LITTLE PIGS

Once upon a time, there were three little pigs who went out into the world to build their homes and seek their fortunes.

The first little pig did not like to work at all. He quickly built his house of straw because that was the

easiest way. Then he danced off down the road to see how his brothers were getting on.

The second little pig was building himself a house, too. He did not like to work either, so he decided to build his house out of sticks. That would be quick and easy. Soon he was finished. The  house made of sticks was not very strong, but at least his work was done. Now he was free to play.

What the second little pig

liked to do best was play his fiddle. The first little pig

played his flute while his brother played the fiddle and

danced. Then the two went off down the road to visit

their brother.

The third little pig was the serious one. He was

building his house out of bricks. He did not mind

working hard, and he wanted his house to be strong. For he knew that in the woods nearby lived a big, bad wolf who liked nothing better than to catch little pigs and eat them! So he worked and

worked, putting each and every brick carefully in place.

The first two pigs laughed when they saw their brother hard at work. But the third little pig just ignored them and carried on building his house. "You can laugh and dance and sing," he called to his brothers. "But I'll be safe and you'll be sorry when the wolf comes to the door!"

The first pig had just reached his house of straw when the wolf came knocking at his door.

"Little pig, little pig, let me come in!" cried the wolf.

"Not by the hair of my chinny-chin-chin!" said the little pig.

"Then I'll huff and I'll puff and I'll blow your house down!" roared the wolf.

And he did. Why, he blew the little straw house to pieces!

The poor little pig ran off to his brother's house made of sticks. Soon, the wolf was at the door. He knew that the little pigs would not let him in, so he disguised himself as a sheep. Luckily the little pigs could see through the wolf's disguise.

"You can't fool us with that sheepskin!" cried the pigs.

"Then I'll huff and I'll puff, and I'll blow your house

down!" yelled the wolf.

And he blew the little house of twigs to pieces!

The two little pigs raced off to their brother's brick house.

"Don't worry," said the third little pig. "You are safe here."

Soon they were laughing and singing again.

This made the wolf very angry. He huffed and he puffed and he puffed and he huffed. But no matter how hard he

tried, he could not blow down that little house of bricks.

The wolf thought and thought about how to get inside.

Ah-ha! He could climb down the chimney. And so he did,

right into a bubbling cauldron of water that the pigs had

hung in the fireplace to cook their dinner.

With a yelp and a scream, the big, bad wolf flew

straight up the chimney and ran off into the woods. The three little pigs never saw him again. They were most content to sing and laugh and dance inside their brother's strong brick house.